D1486604

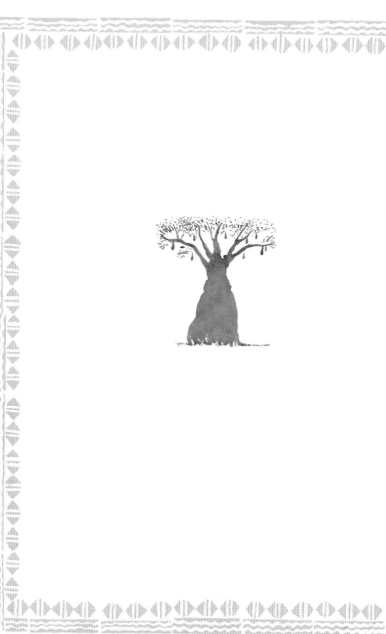

THE
NIGHT
COUNTRY

BRYCE
COURTENAY

WATERCOLOURS BY
STEPHEN FEARNLEY

VIKING

Viking
Penguin Books Australia Ltd
487 Maroondah Highway, PO Box 257
Ringwood, Victoria 3134, Australia
Penguin Books Ltd
Harmondsworth, Middlesex, England
Viking Penguin, A Division of Penguin Books USA Inc.
375 Hudson Street, New York, New York 10014, USA
Penguin Books Canada Limited
10 Alcorn Avenue, Toronto, Ontario, Canada M4V 3B2
Penguin Books (N.Z.) Ltd
Cnr Rosedale and Airborne Roads, Albany, Auckland, New Zealand

First published by Penguin Books Australia Ltd 1998

1 3 5 7 9 10 8 6 4 2

Typeset and design by Tony Palmer, Penguin Design Studio
Printed and bound in Australia by Southbank Press

National Library of Australia
Cataloguing-in-Publication data:

Courtenay, Bryce, 1933–.
The night country.
ISBN 0670 878995.
I. Title.
A823.3

WRITERS' BLOC

THE READER IS ALWAYS RIGHT

For Celeste and Jasper
– Bryce Courtenay

For Frank
– Stephen Fearnley

THE NIGHT COUNTRY

AT THE TAG END of the Great Depression, the three of us, my mother, Marjorie-Ann and I, lived in a single room with a make-shift kitchenette without running water. It was behind a Kaffir shop owned by Mr Polanski.

Everybody else called Mr Polanski's shop 'the Jew Shop', which Ma said was not a nice thing to say about a precious man like Mr Polanski. The shop was in a small town in the Northern Transvaal, a part of South Africa which is usually dismissed by people from other places with a sniff and a superior grin.

I remember how the kindly little Jewish man would speak English to us, but always in a low voice, darting a look over his shoulder after each sentence. It was as though he was afraid of being overheard in this place where English was a forbidden language – where only the *taal* was spoken, the guttural, harsh Afrikaans of the backveld Boers.

That year, our mother was suffering from a severe bout of malaria and lay in a state of delirium in the small, dark room. I was five years old, and my sister Marjorie-Ann was six and a half. We nursed our mother together, covering her body with a wet sheet every hour or so to cool down the malarial furnace that raged within her.

We'd soak the sheet in a large white enamel basin in the backyard. I'd fill the basin with an empty jam tin from a tap set against the back wall of Mr Polanski's shop. We'd dunk the sheet into the basin, punching all the white air pockets back under the water until it was thoroughly soaked. Then I'd take one side and Marjorie-Ann the other and we'd wring the sheet out, holding on tight as anything, twisting until our wrists ached and our fingers lost their strength.

Then we'd carry the sheet, twisted like a liquorice stick, inside to where our mother lay. There we'd untwist it and wrap it around her naked, shivering body. In an hour the sheet would be dry again. How she could be hot enough to dry out a sheet in an hour, and still shiver with her teeth chattering like billyoh at the same time, was a mystery to me. But that's malaria for you.

Whenever Ma came to, I'd lift her head and Marjorie-Ann would put a mug of water to her cracked lips. The mug rattling against her teeth made the water spill over her lip and splash down into the space between her small, flat breasts. Not that this mattered, because she was soaking wet already from sweat, and her hair stuck to her forehead and the nape of her neck.

Once Marjorie-Ann tried to get Ma to take a quinine tablet but it stuck to her dry tongue and stayed there, even when we tried to splash it down her throat with a mug of water.

From early morning the heat beat down on the corrugated iron roof and the room became intensely hot. Bottle flies, blue and bloated, buzzed in and out of the door every time we went into the backyard. When I wasn't filling the basin or helping to wring out the sheet I was swatting flies with a yellow swatter, creeping up on them and . . . blat!

I was too young at the time to understand how we came to be in the small room with my mother dying of malaria. And again, I can't say how long we had been living like this, looking after ourselves, surviving on Marie biscuits and Klim, a brand of powdered milk. Children have no sense of time, so perhaps it was only for four or five days over a holiday period. It seems unlikely that it could have been much longer or, for sure, we would have been discovered by Mr Polanski's dog, Billy.

Billy was a fox terrier who once sat for a whole weekend alone in the shop with his nose resting on a

Marmite cracker because Mr Polanski, who had trained him to eat only after a password was said, hadn't said the password. Billy would come around and visit us from time to time even though we couldn't give him things to eat, because we didn't know the password.

It was morning when the giant came to our house. I'd returned from having a piss in the backyard, where, by the way, I'd traced a perfect figure eight in the plopping red dust at my feet without once getting a drop on my toes. There was a loud knock on the door of the kitchen. I opened the door and looked straight into the moleskin kneecaps of a giant.

The knees moved back two paces as the door opened fully and I was able to look heavenwards.

The giant was looking down at me. He had piercing blue eyes and a waterfall of white hair which cascaded in waves almost to his waist, as white as Father Christmas's beard.

I'd heard some talk about Christmas around our place, but my mother had become so ill the talk had stopped, and Christmas seemed to have gone away. But perhaps Father Christmas was coming to us anyway? I peered again to see if this could be him. The giant straddling the doorway wore no pixie cap puddled on his head, and he would have been mad to wear a red fur-trimmed coat in this heat. Both his hands hung free, so he wasn't carrying a bag of toys over his shoulder.

The beard around the giant's pink mouth was stained yellow from chewing tobacco. His huge hands ended well above my head and his arms, burned black in the sun, were coated with a dense matting of dark hair that stretched back from wrists which were as thick and muscled as Popeye's, or even more so, like those of his arch enemy, the terrible, black-stubbled Bluto.

The giant placed one of his big hands on my head and, looking up, I could see through the gaps in his fingers. It was like standing beside the trunk of a huge tree, looking at the sun's sharp rays through broad, dark branches that smelled of nicotine and engine oil.

Far from being Father Christmas, perhaps this was the giant in 'Jack and the Beanstalk'! In my fear, I heard the words of the storytale echo in my head:

'Fee, fi, fo, fum, I smell the blood of an Englishman!

'Far from being Father Christmas,
perhaps this was the giant in
"Jack and the Beanstalk"!'

'Be he alive or be he dead, I'll grind his bones to make my bread!'

Now the giant removed his hand from my head and spoke to us. It was the first time I'd realised that the giant in 'Jack and the Beanstalk' was an Afrikaner. Marjorie-Ann had come to stand behind me and as neither of us spoke Afrikaans we could not understand the giant. She looked up at him bravely, and, using some of the few Afrikaans words she knew, she said, 'Can you speak English, please, Meneer?'

He paused and pulled his thick pink lips into a straight disapproving line, stretching the yellow tobacco stain around his mouth. Then he cleared his throat, a sound like small boulders rattling in a concrete mixer. When he spoke English, it was as though he was trying to hold down something awful-tasting, like warm boiled beetroot which I hated too.

'Sick? You mama, she sick, ja?'

'Oh, yes, she is going to die,' I said, knowing that death was something that happened to people who became very sick, probably with malaria.

Marjorie-Ann nodded, uncertain what to make of the giant, who now stepped right up to the door so that his head and the top of his shoulders were well above the lintel. An enormous headless presence filled the space around us and gave off the pungent odour of sweat and a second, sweeter smell, of tobacco cured in molasses. The giant's moleskins were strapped by a wide, sweat-oiled leather belt, fixed with a large, square brass buckle at the waist, but his trousers did not end there. They continued up for another six inches, splaying outwards and turning themselves inside out to show a dirty cotton lining. The giant's great tummy sat like an egg within this comfortable-looking nest of soft moleskin.

Suddenly, his hairy calloused hands with their black-rimmed nails swooped towards us, but stopped just short and grasped the trousers above his knees. The giant's legs began to buckle until his shoulders and beard appeared from above the lintel, followed by a great red face topped with a shining bald head.

Close up like this, with his huge frame filling the door space, there was simply no mistaking him. I was one hundred per cent certain that this really *was* the giant out of 'Jack and the Beanstalk'.

Now almost on his haunches, the giant put out a

hand as big as a road worker's shovel and pushed us gently aside. Twisting his shoulders sideways, he forced his body through the small doorway and into the darkened kitchen space beyond.

Once inside, he rose again, his great bald head bumping the tin roof, creating a sharp metallic sound that made the whole room jump. He stooped and rubbed his head briefly before moving to where my mother lay shaking and rattling in her fever.

I was later to learn that the giant stood seven feet and a bit inches tall, and weighed three hundred and twenty-five pounds. He paused for a moment looking down at my mother, running his hand pensively through his beard so that the silver hair seemed to grow like magic out of the top of his fist.

Then he pronounced the single word, 'Malaria.'

He waited, perhaps expecting some sort of response from my mother. But when none came he cleared his throat and introduced himself. 'De Bruin, missus!' Then he added, '*Cornelius* De Bruin,' as though knowing his Christian name would make sense of everything for the delirious woman who lay on the packing case bed at his feet, vacantly staring up at him through fever-bright eyes.

The giant stood for a moment longer. Then he seemed to make up his mind what to do. He wiped the back of his hand across his mouth and bending down, scooped Ma from the bed, the wet sheet still clinging to her naked body. In his great, hairy, sunburned Bluto arms, she seemed to be no larger than a small child.

'You can't eat her! She isn't dead yet,' I said, starting to blub, for I knew that giants ate people.

'Kom, kinder!' he commanded in a huge gruff voice, scurrying us ahead of him with a jerk of his beard. We had few clothes anyway, but we left without them. Perhaps they were fetched later – I don't recall. All I knew was that we'd been captured by a terrible giant, and giants don't wait around while you pack a suitcase.

I gripped Marjorie-Ann's hand tightly and we followed him outside to where a Model T Ford stood parked in the street. The ancient vehicle had been converted into a flat-bed truck. A large African woman sat in the back. Seeing us approach, she stood up to reveal a narrow mattress which occupied about half the width of the truck.

The sight of the black woman cheered me up immediately. As a small child I'd had a Zulu wet nurse and nanny, and I knew that women with large black breasts and smiling white teeth looked after little boys and didn't ever harm or beat them, even when they were bad.

The giant said something to her in Shangaan, and she smiled shyly and removed from around her waist a length of striped, blue cotton ticking which she'd been wearing as an extra skirt.

The woman flapped this cloth once or twice in the air and placed it over the mattress. Then she settled herself on the mattress with her back against the back of the driver's cabin, and her legs curled to one side. And she smiled at me.

The giant leaned over and lay my groaning,

shrouded mother onto the mattress with her head resting on the black woman's soft, generous lap.

The cabin doors on the Model T had been removed and the huge Boer pointed, indicating that Marjorie-Ann and I should climb in. He stretched across us into the cabin and pumped the throttle a few times, leaving it half-way open, then he walked to the front of the little lorry. With a grunting jerk of the radiator crank handle, the engine burst into discordant, shuddering life.

We had seated ourselves on the slippery canvas seat and now the gear stick, resting between Marjorie-Ann's right knee and my left, commenced to vibrate so violently that its black knob became

completely blurred and the entire driver's cabin started to shake. I grabbed onto my sister and we clung to each other as we too began to shake, the vibrating cabin threatening to bounce us right back out into the dusty street.

The giant climbed aboard and pushed the throttle back into the rusty tin dashboard. Then the gear stick and the cabin stopped shaking and rattling, and the engine settled down to a jerky sort of rhythm. In a cloud of blue smoke, and with a series of backfiring noises, we moved away down the empty main street, towards the giant's lair and into captivity.

I had stopped crying but continued to clutch Marjorie-Ann. Weighed down with the responsibility of my mother and me, she hadn't uttered a single word since we'd left the room behind the shop. Once in a while she'd sniff and jerk her head backwards. Her long blonde plaits would bounce against her pretty face and a tear would streak down her cheek and disappear over the edge, into the lap of her dirty, printed cotton dress.

With Marjorie-Ann sniffling like that, I knew we must be in pretty big trouble all right as crying was not her game at all. Like me, she thought we were going to become the giant's Christmas dinner.

But I had not given up hope altogether. The thought of the black woman cheered me up no end. In my book, evil giants didn't keep big, soft, smiling nannies on hand to cut up scrawny little children into bite-sized chunks. My commonsense told me that, to a vicious and cruel giant, she would be a delicious morsel herself and that he would have eaten her long

*'In a cloud of blue smoke, we moved
down the empty road, towards the
giant's lair . . .'*

◀▶◁▷◁▷◁▷ ◁▷◁▷ ◀▶◁▷◁▷◁▷ ◁▷◁▷◁▷

ago. And so I realised that the giant was not a giant at all. He was Oupa De Bruin.

We stayed on Oupa De Bruin's remote farm for more than six months, mixed up with the small sons and daughters of his sons and daughters, and treated no differently from his own grandchildren.

The word 'oupa' simply means grandfather. It soon seemed perfectly natural for us to call him this.

Oupa took no notice of us just as he took no notice of his real grandchildren. And so we ran wild on the farm, coming back to the farmhouse for food and sleep.

Our lives were controlled by Ousis, a word which means 'older sister', but at the same time means much, much more. Ousis was almost as tall as

Oupa De Bruin and probably weighed as much, and she held absolute dominion over us kids.

Ousis had a moustache like a man and she wore her dark hair pulled back and braided around her head. She walked around in bare feet wearing a tent-like faded floral dress, which always seemed clean enough to my eyes, but which she never seemed to change. Perhaps she had lots of them all the same.

Ousis had a very deep, big voice which would bring the little black kitchen maids trembling to her side from just about anywhere on the farm. When she brought her fingers to her lips and whistled, we kids would come running, and the bush doves in the blue gum trees would fly up in fright. But underneath all this was a heart as big as a tractor engine.

Ousis rose at four each morning to bake bread in

the Dutch oven in the yard behind the kitchen. At five she woke the eleven kids who slept in two Victorian brass feather beds in the large, dark room leading onto the back stoep. By the time we stumbled into the kitchen, knuckling the sleep from our eyes, the scrubbed pine table was covered with tin mugs. These were filled with sweet steaming mountain coffee, beside which stood a large basket of rock hard rusks, the result of a week's continuous baking in the autumn. The maids had long since smeared the kitchen floor with fresh cow dung which had dried to a soft khaki-yellow colour, so that each morning smelled of new cut grass and fresh baked bread.

It was Ousis who fed us and admonished us, though her sharp words usually ended in a laugh. It was Ousis who nursed our cuts, painting them with iodine which stung like mad. She also mended the tears in our ragged clothes and sometimes even patched up our quarrels.

At night, we stood in line in the kitchen. Each of us in turn sat on the *riempie* stool and placed our dirty feet into a large tin basin of hot water while one of the maids, kneeling on the floor beside us, gave them a bit of a scrub with a coarse loofah brush. Then they wiped our hands and face with a warm cloth from a separate basin of almost clean water, working the coarse towelling between our fingers, squeezing out the dirt. The maids did not mind about our little cuts and sores, and ignored our winces and ouches and cries of indignation as we were practically murdered every night. After this agony they made us close our eyes as they wiped the dirt from our faces.

*'The paraffin lamp was then turned down
to a thin circle of orange light . . .'*

Lastly, with a flannelled forefinger, they pried the dry, dusty snot from our noses.

It was Ousis who made us kneel beside the two great brass beds each night and say our prayers before she tucked us in. The paraffin lamp was then turned down to a thin circle of orange light, sufficient only to soften the dark so that we would not be fearful of the night or, in our dreams, mistake the babble of the brook which ran past the open window for the cackling laughter of dead Kaffir ghosts.

I would lie very still in the great feather bed under a mosquito net with five other kids asleep around me and listen. Soon, over the babble of water would come a different sound, the soughing of the wind through the huge old blue gum trees which surrounded the farmstead. It was a noise that swept and rushed and whooshed into a leafy kingdom two hundred feet above the hard, baked earth of the farmyard.

This was 'Jack and the Beanstalk' country all right, but Oupa De Bruin hadn't turned out to be even one bit as fearsome as a real giant. Though I have to say, life on the farm wasn't all that much fun at first. I was the smallest of the eight boys there, and although I was learning Afrikaans pretty quickly, it wasn't fast enough. I was a Rooinek, which I soon learned wasn't a very good thing to be. I spoke English. I got beaten up when I didn't know a word in Afrikaans or made the mistake of asking for something in English. While being beaten by the other kids encouraged me to learn a new language, it wasn't doing my confidence a lot of good.

Soon after we'd arrived on the farm, I said something in English and got a bloody nose for my mistake. I sat in the dirt bawling and sniffling, circled by the other kids who laughed and made fun of me. Suddenly a great shadow fell over us and Ousis appeared. She scooped me up into her arms and carried me some distance away until she could sit her huge body, with me almost lost in her lap, on one of the steps leading up to the farmhouse stoep.

She didn't seem to mind that I dripped blood onto her skirt and made no attempt to stop the flow.

'Come skatterbol, you are five years old, this is the last time you may cry. You see, when you cry you make me cry also!' Then Ousis burst into tears so violent that they splashed down her great red cheeks and crashed onto the back of my neck.

This lukewarm waterfall of grief seemed somehow to stop the flow of blood from my nose and I ceased crying at once, unable to compete with her Victoria Falls of blubbing.

'No, no, little boetie, you must cry some more!' Ousis demanded, between great gulping sobs. 'This is the last time! After this you must never cry again. Your mama wrote to say tomorrow you are six. At six a man can't cry any more, you hear?'

Ousis gave another big sob, hugging me to her enormous breasts, and together we cried at the top of our voices. I'm telling you, that was a cry and a half. I roared and I wailed and I sobbed and whimpered and sniffed, but Ousis beat me hands down.

On the day of our arrival at Oupa De Bruin's farm my mother had been taken to Tzaneen hospital, some thirty miles away. I don't remember her leaving us, I only remember that some time later, when she was well enough to leave the hospital, she came back to the farm to grow strong again. She was very thin and a bit dried out, with large black rings around her eyes. Ousis placed her in a rocking chair under the blue gum trees. There she sat beside Oupa De Bruin's old wife, Ouma.

Ouma was much too far gone to be a real grandmother to all us kids. People said she was mad. She never spoke and seemed only to fumble with a brass snuff box and pinch snuff to her nostrils all day long.

Ouma was a sort of wheezing and sneezing machine, a tiny lady dressed in black who wore a shawl over her head. The shawl was red, the only touch of colour in her clothes. We weren't allowed to go too near her and I was to learn from the other children that she had gone mad in the Kaffir Wars because of what the Kaffirs had done to her. It was never explained what this was, but it must have been something pretty terrible to send her wheezing and sneezing and mad all over the place like that.

When you came up to her she'd slowly turn her head and give a high, frightened cackle, shaking her bony finger in your direction. Then she'd bring her tiny white claws up and clutch fearfully at her breast and begin to whimper.

'She thinks you're a Kaffir and are going to do it to her,' one of the other kids would explain. 'The

Kaffirs did it to her a hundred times in the Kaffir Wars, man!'

I was never able to discover what 'it' was, but if Ousis saw you teasing Ouma, or even getting too close to the old woman in her red shawl, she'd give you such a solid clout behind the earhole that her pile-driving arm would send you travelling several yards forward with your nose finally skidding in the dust.

So we had to stay well away from the wheezing old crone who had had it done to her a hundred times.

For Marjorie-Ann and me, this was very traumatic. My mother was sitting next to the old woman, which made it impossible for us to approach her during the day. After a brief kiss at night she always begged us in a thin pleading voice, which didn't sound at all like her old one, to be good and do as we were told because Oupa De Bruin was a precious man.

The other kids decided that because of her proximity to Ouma, she too must be mad and soon their relentless taunting made me believe it was true.

'Your ma is mad! Your ma is mad! Ha, ha, ha, you've got no pa and your ma is mad, mad, mad!' they'd sing, circling around me like hyenas, as I held my hands to my ears, trying to block out those terrible words.

When they grew tired of taunting me, I'd wait until nobody was looking and go to a secret place I'd discovered. It was a small, dark, wattle and daub shed standing some little distance from the farmhouse. The dark, cool hut contained bags of ground corn, known as mealie meal. From its open blue gum rafters hung large yellow leaves of tobacco and a few spikes of dry aloe, which was ground very fine and used as medicine, mixed in Ouma's snuff.

I loved the sweet smell in that shed from the tobacco, tainted with the slightly musty odour which came from the ground corn. It was a sort of comforting aroma that went well with the soft half-light and the business of being alone.

I'd sit on a plump bag of mealie meal, the coarse hessian scratching the backs of my knees. I sat on my own, thinking about malaria and my mother and why people go mad. I even wondered if when Kaffirs 'did it', 'it' first turned into malaria and then into madness. Perhaps the Kaffirs had done it to my mother, although she'd never spoken about being in a Kaffir war. But when I asked Marjorie-Ann she said malaria came from mosquitoes, not Kaffirs.

I worried about what would happen to our poor, thin ma if she was sent to the madhouse as the other kids promised she surely would be. And I worried about what would happen to us – Marjorie-Ann and me – if Ma went to the madhouse. I was a born worrier and the sight of my mother, sitting dozing in the shade in her rocking chair beside Ouma, wasn't all that helpful. Ousis kept saying that Ma was getting better and would soon be her old self again.

I should have believed her too, for Ousis had proved quite right in another matter. Apart from a few stray sniffs, since I turned six it was no longer

possible for me to cry. So I'd just sit and worry a lot and feel pretty miserable. Then I'd hear Ousis hitting the railway sleeper that hung from the branch of an old plum tree outside the kitchen. Ousis used to bang the sleeper with an iron rod to bring us kids in for lunch or dinner when she didn't feel like whistling. And I'd perk up a bit and wander inside. Life has a habit of going on.

In the weeks that followed, my mother grew well again just as Ousis said. She was just like her old self. But before we could get to know her all over again, she had to return to work in Duiwelskloof, the little town where we'd lived behind Mr Polanski's shop. My mother was to leave us on Oupa De Bruin's farm until she could afford to have us back with her again.

Our playmates were not very pleased about my mother getting well. She didn't sit under the blue gum trees next to Ouma anymore. She was not mad, and they had sort of liked having two mad women rocking under the trees – it was much more spooky! For me, though, now that my fears for my mother were gone, life on the farm picked up a whole lot.

Now, more than fifty years later, the impressions of that time wash over each other in no particular sequence. My memories are of soon speaking Afrikaans as well as Shangaan. Of lowing red cattle mulling in a giant kraal formed of twisted, bone-white wood. Of the papery rustle of wind through late summer corn.

Out of nowhere sometimes comes a memory of late mornings, when the heat silenced even the singing of the women picking cotton and the shimmering, glassy air filled up so completely with the shrillness of cicadas that after a while you forgot to hear them and they became the stillness itself.

I can still recall the flat, dry smell of late afternoon heat and the dark, blurred shapes of returning cattle, the bells of the milking cows tinkling softly in the rapidly fading day, and the cries of greeting from the half-seen shapes of naked herd boys in a cloud of beast dust, backlit against a blood-red bushveld sunset.

But of all these memories there is one, one single incident, which changed my life forever.

Let me tell you about the Monkey Man.

Near Oupa De Bruin's farm lies the royal kraal of Modjadji, the Rain Queen. She belonged to the Venda tribe, a people who have never in their history made war on any other tribe and who have only one purpose in life: to bring to their throne a Queen who is placed on earth with the greatest of all powers – the power to make rain.

Nobody knew where these rain people came from. They were thought to have been born near the misty conjunction of two great rivers, when time was an infant and where the gods, who made them especially beautiful and pure, gave them the gift of rain to protect them from the marauding tribes sweeping down from the north.

The Rain Queen and her people lived under the protection of all the tribes. Even the Boers, who had known drought often enough, were not prepared to cast doubt on her magic powers. Too many times they'd heard the royal drums of Modjadji beat out their commands to a brazen, barren sky and then before nightfall the skies would fill with heavy, dark rain clouds, veined with lightning and growling with promising thunder.

There was an unspoken rule among the tribes that Modjadji could only be visited after the dust devils had ridden for three spring seasons across parched lands, and only after the Sangoma witchdoctors, great and small, had exhausted their own powers to make rain. This they would do by casting the bones and lighting a magic fire, watching as the sacred smoke rose into a sky shorn of its fleece of clouds by the angry gods. When, day after day,

'I can still recall the flat, dry smell of late afternoon heat, and the dark, blurred shapes of returning cattle, the bells of the milking cows tinkling softly in the rapidly fading day . . .'

month after month, despite their powerful incantations and magic spells, the sky still stretched smooth and blue as skimmed milk above their thirsty lands, only then would the Sangomas pack away the knuckle bones of the sacred white ox and admit that their power was not enough to break open the stubborn sky.

'It is time to go to her. Only she can reach the gods now, and please them with her voice and beauty and cunning female ways,' they would tell the chiefs and tribal elders. Then they would begin to make preparations for the journey to the north to make a supplication to Modjadji, the greatest of all women. Her throne sat on a majestic golden cloud which only a Sangoma who had prepared his rituals correctly could see with magic eyes.

The people of the tribe would understand that this particular drought, this particular sky, could only be broken if certain steps were followed. Their witchdoctor had to choose his omens carefully and arrive at the royal kraal of Modjadji at the propitious time, when the day moon was full and white in the sky. Only then after supplication to the Rain Queen would the drums of Modjadji begin to beat, their rhythm picked up and repeated exactly by the drums of the other tribes, to the very shadow of a single beat, carrying the sound over the earth until finally it reached the parched lands of the supplicant tribe, even a thousand miles away.

Soon puffs of cloud like early morning breath would appear. Then, cotton clouds, strung across the horizon like herds of grazing, pure white goats, after

'Then, cotton clouds, strung across the horizon,
after which would follow great towering cliffs
and mountains of tumbling air . . .'

THE NIGHT COUNTRY

[44]

which would follow great towering cliffs and mountains of tumbling air filled with moisture. Often, on the very day nominated by the great Queen, the rains came, huge splashes that struck down at an angle and smacked into the earth and kicked up the dust and then roared into a fury, turning the parched soil into roiling red mud to be carried thundering down dry creek beds, the rushing, gorgeous blood of Modjadji's generous gift.

In respect of rain, it was known from the beginning of time that Modjadji's power was greater by far than the greatest of the witchdoctors. Soothsayers and medicine men who held tens of thousands of people in awe would kneel humbly at the feet of the young Queen and speak with reverence in a voice not above a hoarse whisper.

The Monkey Man had come to do the same, for the clouds had not gathered for three seasons above the peaks and kranse of the high Drakensberg and there was a great and lingering drought in Zululand.

The Monkey Man, who, I learned from the kitchen maids, was a powerful and famous witchdoctor, must somehow have been known to Oupa De Bruin. Perhaps he was summoned. All I know is that he appeared on the farm on an afternoon two days after a terrible crisis had occurred.

A four-gallon tin of paraffin and a hurricane lamp had been stolen from the storehouse behind the kitchen. This was an unthinkable thing to have happen. Nothing on the farm was ever locked; stealing was simply not even imagined as the punishment would be anything the mind could dream of, or even worse.

Nevertheless, the paraffin and the lamp were missing. While all the servants and farm labourers had been paraded outside the house and the thief given until morning to replace the stolen goods, nothing had as yet happened.

It was also unthinkable that someone other than one of the farm labourers or servants was responsible, as no strange African would be able to put a foot on the property without being spotted. The culprit, we gathered from the grown-ups, was definitely some *verdomde* Kaffir on the farm.

The Monkey Man drove up to the house in a 1936 Buick. You might think that such a car would denote his status as one of the great witchdoctors of

Africa, as well as a man of enormous wealth. But in this part of the world it counted for little. He was still a Kaffir, a heathen, a child of evil and a nobody, even less than a nobody, because he was made by the devil and created, so people said, in the likeness of an aging monkey.

The great witchdoctor was less than four feet in height with a big hump on his back, and so old that his stoop brought his head almost to his knees. His arms dangled as he walked and he seemed to mutter and jabber constantly. The old man's hair and beard were snowy white and grew in a great fuzzy bush around his tiny face, his rheumy eyes the colour of diluted blood.

To me the Monkey Man was a frightening sight. I didn't hesitate to believe in his awesome powers.

People muttered the words 'dirty old Kaffir' around him, but he wasn't someone you would throw stones or shout at. The Monkey Man wore the traditional leopard skin which hung from his shoulders to the ground and carried a beautifully beaded fly switch of horse hair. As he walked he jerked his head from side to side, taking everything in, even though his head seemed no more than a couple of feet above the ground and he had to look up, even at me.

I felt quite sure that the Monkey Man could look directly into my wicked, frightened heart if he wanted to and put his tiny black claw through my chest, tear out my heart and examine it, sniff it, shake his head in disgust and throw it into the dust. For even at my young age I felt a palpable guilt, a guilt of white skin and blue eyes. I felt a guilt about the way I was expected to think of the dark people around me.

That night the little black kitchen maids who washed our feet and hands told us that Oupa De Bruin had paid the great umNgoma to find out who had stolen the paraffin and the hurricane lamp. Their eyes grew large and astonished as they talked of this, knowing that it was impossible for the culprit to escape the trap the mighty umNgoma would set for him. The Monkey Man's powers were so great, they said, that the thief was doomed. He would surely die, possibly even before morning, without the great man laying a bony claw on him or even seeing him face to face.

Late the next morning, when the sun beat down

on the farmyard, all the servants and farm labourers were again paraded outside the farmhouse.

Oupa De Bruin stood watching, with his great sjambok. He tapped the thick, malevolent-looking, five-foot plaited leather whip against his moleskins while the Monkey Man screeched at all the men to stand in a straight line in front of him.

When they had assembled in a more or less straight line, the Monkey Man ordered them all to hold out their left arms, palms upwards. This done, the tiny wizard hopped from one black man to the next, taking small pebbles from a leather bag tied around his neck. Stretching up, he placed a pebble on the palm of each man.

We all watched. Would a particular hand begin to shake with guilt as the magic pebbles started to vibrate? Or would one pebble glow red hot, and burn a sizzling, flesh-plopping hole right through the pale yellow palm of the thief, to emerge, like the pip of a boil, from the dark underside? So many hands were shaking in terror at the mere prospect of being accused that this was obviously not the way to discover the culprit.

Next, the Monkey Man built a tiny fire of grass and chicken feathers, sprinkling it with a powder that made the flames turn blue and flare up and the smoke rise from the fire into a thin, dense white column. He waved his hands though the smoke as though he was gathering it up and then rubbed the captured whisps into his face, his tiny darting tongue shooting in and out, rapidly licking at the air, making a strange high-pitched sound. Now the smoke he'd moments before

*'The Monkey Man built a fire of grass
and chicken feathers, sprinkling it with a
powder that made the flames turn blue
and flare up . . .'*

swallowed started to come out of his ears. This we saw with our own eyes.

After a minute or so, when the fire had died down, the Monkey Man patted the ashes and spread them into a circle about two feet in diameter. Seated on his haunches, he withdrew pieces of the shin bone of the great white ox from another ancient leather bag which hung around his neck. He tossed the bits of bone, one at a time, so that they each landed with a tiny plop of dust and ash within the circle.

The little wizened man sat watching the bones, groaning and keening from time to time as he rocked; then he would flick one of the tiny bone fragments, sending it spinning out of the circle. Growling and chattering to himself, he'd hop over to where it landed, watch it carefully for a moment, then pounce, scoop it up and swallow it. He shook his head and the marble-sized bit of bone disappeared like a worm down a turkey's throat.

When all the pieces of bone were inside his stomach, he rose and moved over to a live chicken which lay with its legs trussed a short distance away from the ash circle. He then produced a pocket knife from his leather bag. It was an old knife with a handle that looked like mother of pearl but was really celluloid, the kind you could buy at any Kaffir store as cheap as anything. Holding the chicken by the head, its beak clasped shut in his tiny hand, he went to the circle and slit its throat over the ashes. A bright gush of blood splashed onto the shiny breast feathers of the wildly fluttering bird before spraying a shower of vivid crimson into the air.

'A bright gush of blood splashed onto the shiny breast feathers of the wildly fluttering bird before spraying a shower of vivid crimson into the air.'

Eventually the chicken stilled to an occasional convulsive jerk. The Monkey Man swung it in an arch several times, then released it, hurling it over his shoulder. The chicken's head remained in his hand as the carcass flew high into the air, with the blood spouting from its open throat falling on two of the Africans standing in line.

There was a loud moan as the chicken landed lifeless in the dust. Then all eyes turned to look at the two men who had been marked with chicken blood.

The faces of both were terrible: their teeth began to chatter and their bodies shook violently. One of them started to howl like a jackal. But neither moved from the line, their hands still containing the tiny pebble held quaking in front of them.

The Monkey Man dropped the chicken's head inside the circle on the ground and, turning slowly, spoke in Shangaan, shouting so all could hear his shrill voice. By now I had begun to understand the language quite well, as it is not so very far removed from Zulu which I'd learned at my nanny's breast. This is what he said to the two blood-splattered men.

'You two are too stupid to be the thieves. The blood has marked you innocent. You may step out of the line.'

Turning away from the two men whom we had all felt certain must be guilty, the Monkey Man looked at the rest of the farm labourers and started to cackle. We could see his few remaining teeth, wet and yellow in his old mouth.

'Ha! Your hands have stopped shaking. When you saw the blood fall on your brothers you gained courage, but it is among you, not them, that I will find the guilty ones!'

Almost immediately several hands began to shake all over again. The old man pointed his finger in the direction of the line of men, running it slowly along to include them all.

'Your fear is indecent, but then you are only of the Shangaan people. You are born cowards whose mothers made love to a hyena so that now you can eat only the flesh that the Zulu lion has blooded and killed for you.'

A desperate moan came from the men, who were already in fear and shock. The Monkey Man looked again at the two men who'd been bloodied by the chicken and who now stood out of the line. 'Go, be off with you!' he screeched at them. Turning their backs on us, they ran for their lives, disappearing into a field of ripe mealies. We could hear them crashing willy-nilly among the corn stalks as they ran.

Oupa De Bruin and the other grown-ups, and of course we kids, thought this was very funny and we laughed a lot. Even I could see the joke. Despite their own fear even some of the black men in the line started to laugh. But I couldn't see what they had to laugh about; they were up to their eyeballs in trouble.

The witchdoctor started to cackle as well, hopping from one leg to another in a crazy jig, his hands on his hips. He laughed and laughed, his shrill cackle growing higher and higher until all the whites stopped laughing and watched him, bemused. Then, as quickly as he'd started, he stopped and walked stiff-legged over to the circle containing the chicken head and blood mixed with the ash from his magic fire.

Straddling the circle, he bent low so that his face was only about eight inches from the ground. One after another, the bones fell from his mouth and rolled into a perfect circle surrounding the chicken head. Its once beady eye was now shut in death by a deep purple eyelid. Tiny sugar ants were already crawling around the half-open beak.

The Monkey Man began to dance around the circle. As though he was playing a game of marbles, he would stop and flick at a tiny bone, sending it shooting at high speed, bouncing and running in the dirt in the direction of the men. He continued doing this until all the small shin bone pieces lay scattered across the line of Africans.

We all understood the ploy, or so we thought. The guilty ones would be where the bones landed. But we were wrong again. The Monkey Man made himself as tall as he could and announced, 'You must have no fear. Only they who are guilty will be found. The tasting of the pebble will make you innocent. I will come to each of you and as I do, you will put the pebble you are holding into your mouth, suck it for a moment, then spit it back into my hand.'

He walked to the far end of the row. Each man did as he was instructed, first placing the pebble in his mouth then, after a moment, spitting it into the witchdoctor's outstretched claw, which was stained with blood. As each pebble landed in his palm, the old man would examine it briefly before dropping the wet rock in the dust at his feet, whereupon he would say, *'ngazi luTho olubi'*, declaring the spitter innocent.

The pressure was unbearable. Nearly three-quarters of the way along the line he examined a pebble in his hand and then snatched at the ragged shirt of the young man in front of him, pulling him from the line. The boy, for he was hardly yet a man, dropped to his knees, quivering all over as he cowered in the dust, his face cupped in his hands.

The Monkey Man seemed not to notice him and continued along the line, accepting and examining each pebble as it landed in his hand. A little further on he repeated the snatch, pulling a second young black man from the line. He too dropped to the ground and began to howl for mercy. Pointing to the first young man, he sobbed that he'd made him do it.

Finally the Monkey Man came to the end of the line and continued walking away without saying a word or even glancing at Oupa De Bruin or at the two young men grovelling and snivelling in the dust. They grabbed handfuls of dirt which they threw over their heads, so that their peppercorn hair and faces were soon covered in red earth.

Oupa De Bruin commanded the two guilty boys to come to him and they rose and went to where he stood, then fell cowering at his feet. He bent down and ripped the ragged shirts from their backs and, rising, drew his sjambok lightly over their naked spines so that they twitched in fright. He asked them quietly in Shangaan where the stolen paraffin and lamp were hidden. The two young men rose to their knees and brought their hands together in front of their faces. Their bodies shaking uncontrollably, they told him.

Oupa De Bruin placed his boot in turn on the shoulders of each at his feet and pushed them over so that they sprawled in the dirt and lay still, not daring to move, though their hopeless weeping could be heard by all of us.

The huge Boer, leaving the culprits where they lay, walked several paces from them and began to speak to the remaining men. His voice seemed somehow different to the one he used on the farm. Now a booming, stentorious sound came from his bearded mouth, as though he was a great prophet, an Elijah preaching the wrath of God.

'You are the devil's children, the sons of Ham!' Now Oupa indicated the whites who stood slightly behind him. 'And *we* are the sons and daughters of the Father of Heaven.' He ran his finger down the line of men, his eyes taking in each one. 'It is not possible for you to steal from us, you hear? Escape from our punishment, from God's punishment, cannot be.'

Then his voice grew lower, though at the same time it seemed to grow more angry. 'You all know I will not call the police. We will not have the police on this farm so that my good name is associated with

Kaffirs who steal!' He spat into the dust at his feet. 'Who steal the bread from my table! I will not permit this shame upon my people. I will punish these devil Kaffirs myself, you hear?'

A terrible moan rose along the line, but many of the black heads nodded in agreement. Oupa De Bruin sighed, speaking in an almost sad voice. 'It is God's will and God's way.' Then he spoke to Ousis. 'Take the women away and the girls too, but let the men and the boys stay. They must see how God's justice works.'

I watched Marjorie-Ann and Ousis and the others trail away through the dirt. I wanted to go with them, but I had to stay.

Oupa De Bruin waited until the women had returned to the farmhouse. Then he walked over to

'I was never to forget that single, terrible moment when the first of a hundred cuts of the sjambok landed . . .'

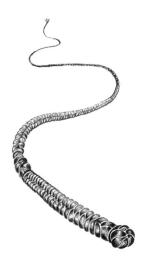

the first African and, grabbing him by the leather strap which held up his ragged trousers, he lifted the man from the ground and carried him forward so that the everyone could see him. Then he dropped the young man on his stomach over an old sawn-off blue gum tree, so that his right hand hung from the side of the stump. The remainder of his torso and left hand lay spread upon it, his legs hanging down over the end.

The youth's slender black body occupied only half of the great stump. Oupa De Bruin returned to the second African and lifted him up in the same manner before dropping him, too, onto the smooth flat stump. His left arm hung from the opposite side of the stump and his dark knuckles touched the ground. Then Oupa lifted the left and right arms of the two Africans and crossed them so that the two men lying on their bellies had their arms around the top half of each other's back.

I was never to forget that single, terrible moment when the first of a hundred or maybe a thousand cuts of the sjambok landed and I saw the flesh torn open on a human back. I looked at the two men lying there together and realised I did not even know their names.

Oupa De Bruin went to work with the whip, landing it expertly, cutting it deep into the shoulder joint of first one man's arm and then the other. The force of the blows echoed among the gum trees as the white giant cut through the skin and layer of fat into the flesh, ripping it open, exposing the gristle and finally the bone. As each blow landed, the man gave a horrible noise, at first a scream and later, after many blows, a cry, fading to a whimper as they lost strength.

Oupa De Bruin stopped only when the sjambok had cut through the flesh and sinew and smashed apart the shoulder joints of both arms, leaving bloody stumps where strong arms had once been joined to the top of strong shoulders.

Both men were unconscious long before this happened and the blue gum stump was splashed and the hard earth at its base was red with their blood. Nobody stirred in the line of black men, nor did any of the whites move from where they stood.

Only I, the weak-stomached Rooinek, was unable to contain my horror. I ran away to my secret place. In the shed I lay retching, my body slumped over a sack of mealie meal.

I kept very still, but my heart was beating like a frightened bird, and then there was a warm feeling around my crotch. I had pissed my pants. My piss, draining through the hessian, soaked into the mealie meal inside.

I had seen the sjambok, the fierce serpent of leather, land with the weight and fury of a seven foot, three hundred-pound giant behind it. I had watched, trembling, as it split bone and splashed blood and bits of human flesh onto Oupa De Bruin's moleskins, until they were soaked from his waist to his knees with the black men's blood.

Later I heard that Ousis had ordered the unconscious bodies of the two men brought to her so that she could stem the blood and clean their ragged shoulders before the heat and flies caused infection.

How long I stayed in the dark cool shed I cannot say. I had taken off my pants and spread them on a sack of meal to dry and then I sat naked on an adjacent sack, my eyes closed, the terrible sjambok sounding still in my head, down my throat and deep into my guts where it echoed worse even than the echoes through the blue gum trees.

After a while I became aware that I was not alone. I opened my eyes to see the Monkey Man squatting a few feet away, staring at me.

'They tell me you speak Zulu, white boy?'

I nodded, terrified, covering my private parts at the sight of the tiny black man.

'Then you and I will speak Zulu. You are not truly of the amabhunu, the Boer, for you cry for the wrong skin.'

I was still too scared to move or speak. He looked down at my hands. 'Take away your hands, this is not a part to shame you. There is no shame in being naked – all Zulu *umfana* at your age are naked, it is how they should be, it is proper.'

It was an instruction to be obeyed and I quickly took away my hands. 'Yes, you are not amabhunu,' he said again, looking at my circumsised penis. I nodded, admitting that I wasn't a Boer, my eyes wide with fear, as I listened to the Monkey Man.

'I have thrown the bones and I have seen you in the smoke and now I must teach you where to hide, so that when you are afraid or lack courage you can

go to where you can still the fear and be brave again.'
He pulled his head to one side, looking at me
through his bloodshot eyes. 'Will you listen to me,
white boy?'

I had not heard Zulu spoken since we'd left
Natal when I'd lost my beautiful big nanny, a time
long ago. The words spoken by the Monkey Man
were in my nanny's language, and she had never
done anything to me that wasn't good. I nodded to
the old man, beginning to feel a little braver.

'Ha! I think you are a white Zulu,' he laughed.
He held up his fly switch, the handle of which was
embroidered in an elaborate pattern of tiny coloured
beads. 'Watch!'

He grasped the fly switch by the horse hair so
that the brightly beaded handle hung down. Slowly

he began to swing the handle like a pendulum. 'Watch the beads, watch them sway like an old woman's buttocks,' he cackled. 'Sway, sway, watch them sway as she goes on her way. *Sway, sway, sway* . . .' His voice was growing slower and lower. 'She goes to gather water in a great clay pot, *sway, sway, sway*, to cook her husband mealie pap and serve it steaming hot! *Sway, sway, sway*. Now count aloud the number of all of your fingers on both of your hands. *Sway, sway, sway* . . .'

I began to count to ten. 'Slowly, count slowly and when you reach ten close your eyes, but slowly,' the Monkey Man instructed.

I began to count again, watching the sweep of the handle which was now a soft blur of colour before my eyes. My eyelids seemed to grow heavy.

*'I lay in the dark, cool shed, the terrible
sjambok sound still in my head, where it
echoed worse than the echoes through
the blue gum trees.'*

Reaching ten, I closed them gratefully. 'Now count ten again, but this time backwards. When you reach the number of one you will be asleep, little white man who mourns over the blood from a black man's back. You will be in the Night Country.'

I began to count down from ten but I don't recall if I ever made it back to one. 'See how you sit at the mouth of a dark cave and overlook this place. If you look beyond it, look into the far distance beyond your eyes, you will see the great water.

'The great water rests beyond the Limbombo Mountains. It is the time of the setting sun. Now you see the sun as it enters into the great dark wetness, its golden fire quenched. Now see again, it is gone only a monent and immediately it begins to rise once more, see how it rises silver from the water, the moon over the Night Country. It is here you can come whenever you are sad, or frightened. It is here where you can re-think your courage and find the way to go and the path to take. It is here where you can meet your shades and speak to them. They are the spirits of your ancestors – they will be your guides.'

I could hear his voice clearly as I sat cross-legged outside a small cave. Below me stretched Oupa De Bruin's farm. I could hear the swoosh of the wind through the blue gum trees and see the small, dark shape of Ouma in her rocking chair. Then I looked further, beyond the bone-white kraal and across the corn fields and I seemed to lose my sight, when a new landscape formed inside my head.

Stretching away from me was a dark, flat, watery firmament that filled the entire space in front of me, as though I was suspended directly in line with the horizon. As the old man spoke, a great fiery orb dropped from above and plunged into the ink dark horizon, like a bright new copper penny dropped into the slot of a money box. There was no splash, no sound at all, simply a huge golden ball disappearing into the black line etched against a barely lighter sky.

I could see it begin to rise from the water again. The world around me filled with a light almost as clear as daylight and below me appeared the farm once more, bathed in moonlight. The shadows of the trees splashed across the settled dust of the farmyard, the glint of the brook crossing it. But no farmhouse. Oupa De Bruin's home was gone.

In its place, rising out of the red dust, were two black arms ending in fists clenched to the sky. Beyond them I could see the great blue gum stump, its silver-grey colour washed clean, as though it were some sacrificial altar now used only by the ghosts of men long since gone.

'You may come back here to the Night Country whenever you wish by closing your eyes and sitting very still, and by the counting of ten, frontways and backways,' said the Monkey Man. 'This place will always be yours, little white boy who has tears enough for a black man's mourning.'

His voice faded and I opened my eyes to find I was alone in the cool, dark shed, seated cross-legged on top of a bag of mealie meal, my hands quietly resting in my lap. I could smell the pungent tobacco leaf hanging from the rafters above me, mixed with the damp, musty aroma of the crushed corn. Outside I heard the solitary schwark of a hen complaining to herself about the midday heat.

I did not see the Monkey Man again and I was too afraid to ask when he'd departed in his big black Buick. But that night as I lay in bed listening like I always did to the wind beyond the water, I discovered that by following his teachings I could return to the Night Country.

Years later, when I'd won a scholarship to a posh boys' school which would otherwise have been well beyond the means of our family, I was mucking around in the biology lab library late one afternoon. Leafing through a book on human behaviour for an essay I needed to write, I finally worked out the secret of the pebbles.

Fear had completely dried up the saliva in the two guilty men's mouths. The pebbles they spat into the Monkey Man's little hand were the only two which were completely dry. Fear is like that: it starts in a dry mouth and it works its way down through the inside of a man and everything it touches dries up, so that finally even the soul shrivels away and a man consumed by fear is as good as dead.

When I decided to find a new land as far from Africa as possible, I carried with me the memory of two severed arms left to lie on a blood-soaked tree stump.

For me those two dark arms, crossed on a makeshift butcher's block, remain the true symbol of apartheid.

Through the use of the pebbles, the Monkey Man had picked the two thieves, who would each lose an arm in the name of the white man's god, a white man's truth and a white man's justice.

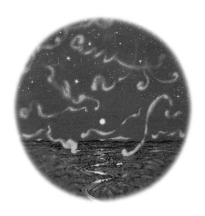

Epilogue: Africa

IT WAS SUNSET, NO, even a little further on towards dark; that space between light and night when the eye can no longer be trusted. The old people say this is the time when the ghosts come out to stretch and yawn. A dangerous time in the bushveld, when thirsty animals come to drink and hungry claws wait to tear at bloody meat.

I climbed a small *koppie*, no more than thorn bush and a pile of rocks in shadow, overlooking a muddy drinking hole three metres across. It was the kind of water that disappears as the summer lengthens. Already the shrink was iron-dry on its outer edges. Closer in, it was pocked and dented with the spoor of game and the sluice marks of elephant and rhino.

Seated above the wind and on the highest rock, I waited.

The sky melted down and the light went out in the west, and almost at once an impatient moon, gossamer thin and not yet turned to the solid gold of proper night, rose up in the eastern sky.

The moon in Africa climbs quickly, scuttling above the silhouettes of flat-topped thorn trees and up into a star-pricked sky. In a moment, there it was, trapped in the centre of the waterhole.

And then, from a high thicket of white thorn and wild palm a giraffe emerged, a ghost shape in the moonlight. It moved with great rocking strides up to the waterhole where it stood a moment, then collapsed its front legs like a folding chair. Its elegant neck, a slender stem darker than the night, craned down and over and sipped from the silver bowl of the moon.

Bryce Courtenay is the best-selling author of
The Power of One, *Tandia*, *A Recipe for Dreaming*,
April Fool's Day, *The Potato Factory* and
Tommo & Hawk.

Stephen Fearnley is an artist, film-maker
and ceramicist living in Sydney.